Frazzle's Fantastic Day

by Deborah Kovacs • Illustrated by Richard Brown

Featuring Jim Henson's Sesame Street Muppets

A SESAME STREET/GOLDEN PRESS BOOK
Published by Western Publishing Company, Inc.
in conjunction with Children's Television Workshop.

Library of Congress Catalog Card Number: 80-83289
ISBN 0-307-23123-2

This is Frazzle.
Frazzle is a nice red monster.
He loves to play make-believe.

But sometimes he makes believe so hard
that he doesn't see what's really happening
around him.

Frazzle decided to build a great big building.
What do you think happened?

Frazzle pretended he was an airplane pilot.
He flew his airplane all around Sesame Street.

What do you
think happened?

Now Frazzle pretended that he was a lion tamer
in the circus. He was teaching the biggest,
meanest lion how to roll over.

What do you think happened?

After that, Frazzle made believe he was riding on a surfboard. He pretended that he was riding the crest of a great big wave.

What do you think happened?

Then Frazzle pretended to be a baker.
He made a beautiful make-believe cake.

What do you think happened?

Frazzle decided to take a bath.

Frazzle pretended he was a tugboat captain.
There was a terrible storm at sea.
The waves got higher...
and higher...
and higher!

What do you think happened?

Frazzle was tired after his busy day.
"Monsters will be monsters!" said his mommy,
as she kissed him goodnight.

What do you think happened?